Mann Hyung Hur graduated from Konkuk University in Seoul, Korea, and earned a Ph.D. in public policy at the University of Colorado at Denver, USA. He is currently a professor at Chung-Ang University, Seoul, Korea.

He has published a novel entitled *Cyber Beatrice* in Korea in 1995, which was the beginning of his professional writing career. He was invited to write serialized stories in the *Digital Times* and *Weekly Donga* in Korea. In addition to novels, he has also published more than ten nonfiction books. *Beyond the Division* has been excerpted from the serialized story collection *Nine Stairs@Omega* and rewritten into a novella.

I would like to dedicate this story to North Korean defectors around the world and children currently living in poverty in North Korea.

Mann Hyung Hur

BEYOND THE DIVISION

AUSTIN MACAULEY PUBLISHERS™
LONDON • CAMBRIDGE • NEW YORK • SHARJAH

Copyright © Mann Hyung Hur (2019)

The right of Mann Hyung Hur to be identified as author of this work has been asserted by him in accordance with section 77 and 78 of the Copyright, Designs and Patents Act 1988.

All rights reserved. No part of this publication may be reproduced, stored in a retrieval system, or transmitted in any form or by any means, electronic, mechanical, photocopying, recording, or otherwise, without the prior permission of the publishers.

Any person who commits any unauthorized act in relation to this publication may be liable to criminal prosecution and civil claims for damages.

A CIP catalogue record for this title is available from the British Library.

ISBN 9781788480697 (Paperback)
ISBN 9781788480703 (Hardback)
ISBN 9781528960724 (ePub e-book)

www.austinmacauley.com

First Published (2019)
Austin Macauley Publishers Ltd
25 Canada Square
Canary Wharf
London
E14 5LQ

Ames, surrounded by endless cornfields, was a desolate city in Iowa. The surrounding countryside was not pretty at all. I felt as if I had been abandoned in the wilderness and so lonesome during my six-month sabbatical leave in the city last year. A part of me always felt empty. I had to find something to fill my emptiness. At that very moment, a girl flashed through my mind. She was the protagonist of this novella, *Beyond the Division*. Soon is a fictional character, but I actually met such a figure during my one-day visit to the North's border city of Gaeseong in 2006.

This novella narrates a forbidden love in a divided Korea and delivers a message of reconciliation, peace, and reunification for the two Koreas. Hundreds of thousands of separated families have been waiting for reunions for over 70 years since the division of the peninsula in 1945. I want this story to be a glimmer of hope for those waiting for the day when the border disappears and a forbidden love in a divided Korea can be realized.

I am greatly indebted to Zachary Lisabeth and Sarah Hagen for their time and effort to copyedit my work. I am also deeply indebted to Professors Mack Shelley, David Russell, and Barbara Hass for their help.

Mann Hyung Hur
Seoul, Korea
May 2018

Table of Contents

Episode 1 11
A White Sheet

Episode 2 21
A Shadow

Episode 3 31
A Tailing

Episode 4 42
A Rhapsody of the Tumen River

Episode 5 53
A Mata Hari Training

Episode 6 64
A Reunion

Episode 1
A White Sheet

PILSUNG met her for the first time at Seonggyungwan – the foremost educational institution in Korea during the Koryo Dynasty (918–1392) – in the North's border city of Gaeseong. She looked so pretty in her Korean traditional outfit. Her neckline was especially attractive, showing off a slim figure. His heart started to pound when he realized she was approaching. A pair of giant gingko trees, hundreds of years old, stood dignified in the institution's extensive yard. Their leaves had turned yellow and some of them were starting to fall on the ground. The wind carried them, rustling.

"Gingko trees... so magnificent!" He started the conversation with her in a quivering voice.

She replied, "Of course, they are! Gingko leaves in the fall are so beautiful. Look at the golden ginkgo trees. You know what? These trees are even more majestic because they stand in *old* Seonggyungwan!"

"What do you mean *old* Seonggyungwan?"

"Oh, I suppose you don't know. I mean Seonggyungwan in Seoul is young. Seonggyungwan in Gaeseong is hundreds of years older than Seonggyungwan in Seoul." She spoke in typical North Korean intonation, showing a typical North Korean pride against South Korea.

A variety of souvenir stalls awaited the customers outside of the main gate of Seonggyungwan. Pilsung and the woman made their way toward the souvenir stalls across the yard. While they were walking, a silence fell between them.

"Hey!" Pilsung broke the silence and brought up a word. She turned her face toward him. Her cheeks flushed for a second. A spark also flashed in her eyes as Pilsung fixed his eyes on hers.

"Recommend a souvenir of North Korea for me, please."

"Sure!"

She quickly looked around the stalls and walked ahead with pride. He followed her. They passed by liquor tables and oriental medicine mats. She didn't pay attention to oriental paintings drawn by a famous North Korean artist at all. She finally stopped walking in front of a book stall.

"Are you interested in buying a book?"

"A book?"

She picked up a book before Pilsung gave his consent. He got closer to her. Her delicate smell wafted through the air. He touched her shoulder with his upper arm accidentally. Once again, his heart started to pound faster and his breathing became more labored. The book in her hand was titled *A Legendary Story of the Songak Mountain*. She handed it to him. He thought for a moment, pulled out a pen from his pocket, and opened the first page of the book in front of her.

"Would you sign here for me, please?"

She stared at him with a smile and nodded her head. He could see her hand trembling a little while she wrote her words:

'I am pleased to meet you. Soon Sul'.

Her name was Soon. Surname? It was Sul. He was so pleased to have her handwritten words in the book. He softly touched her words on the page several times and put it in his backpack with loving care.

She led him to Sunjukgyo, a stone bridge built in 1290. Jeong Mongju (1337–1392), a famous loyal advisor to the last king of the late Koryo Dynasty, was assassinated by a newly emerging power of the Chosun Dynasty (1392–1910) on this bridge. As a Confucian scholar, Jeong Mongju stood firm in his view that a faithful subject should not serve two kings.

"Do you know Jeong Mongju?" Soon asked with a smile on her face.

"Yes, I do," Pilsung nodded.

"What about his poem, *A Song of Single-Hearted Loyalty*? Can you recite it?" She looked at him with inquisitive eyes.

"Of course, I can recite the poem! I had to perform it countless times throughout elementary school, middle school, and high school."

"Oh, yeah? I remember doing that, too. Shall we recite the poem together?"

"Sure! Let's do that," Pilsung nodded, staring at her eyes.

"I will start with the first line. You do the second line. And then we recite the last line together. How do you like that plan?"

"Excellent!"

Soon cleared her throat several times and stared at Pilsung with her lovely eyes as she recited the first line. "*Even though I die, die again, and more than hundred times I die.*"

Pilsung followed with the second line, still watching Soon's eyes, "*Although my body turns to dust and dirt, whether my soul remains or not.*"

Soon nodded her head in rhythm to Pilsung's recitation. She touched Pilsung's hand, sending him a slight signal. The two recited the last line at the same time, "*My single-hearted loyalty to my lover will not change forever.*"

They crossed the bridge while they spoke. The two shadows of Pilsung and Soon grew longer as the sun set.

"How do you like the poem?" she asked crossing the bridge back toward Seonggyungwan.

"Um…" Pilsung opened his mouth to answer the question, but she continued before Pilsung spoke out a word.

"It's one of my favorite poems. I like the last line very much. *My single-hearted loyalty to my lover will not change forever.* I love it so much." She recited it softly a couple times and looked at Pilsung with a smile. They kept walking slowly toward a bus waiting to depart for Seoul.

Pilsung couldn't put her out of his mind after he came back from the short trip to Gaeseong, North Korea. He tried to forget her so many times, but he couldn't. Her voice speaking the last line of Jeong Mongju's poem – *My single-*

hearted loyalty to my lover will not change forever – lingered, the image of her speaking poetry forever burned into his mind. He couldn't sleep.

He fell seriously ill for a while. He could not wake up from the fever until he made a decision on finding his job at the Gaeseong Industrial Complex, a symbol of inter-Korea cooperation. For him, it was a little, but his only, hope to see her again.

YEOOK hadn't slept well in recent months. The possibilities of a permanent shutdown of the Gaeseong Industrial Complex had been hanging over her head. Her sewing factory in Gaeseong was all she had, and all she had accomplished so far in her life. She was afraid of losing it in a single day. One sunny day, she decided to visit the Odusan Unification Observatory, the northernmost point overlooking the North Korean border. She seemed to recover her psychological stability by doing so. She asked Pilsung to go with her. While she drove her car, she glimpsed at Pilsung in the passenger seat.

His eyes were a bit bloodshot and wet with tears, like they were on the day he moved out of Gaeseong with a fully loaded truck. The moment when she saw the truck parked in front of her office in Seoul, she felt as if her entire life was being destroyed. She wouldn't leave her office on that evening. She stayed around and looked out the window for hours. It was around midnight when a knock sounded on her office. Pilsung stuck his head in the door.

"Sister…" He called his boss sister. "…I feel so bitter because I can't see Soon any more. Will I be able to see her again?" He stared at Yeook and feebly lowered his head.

"Who did you say? Soon?"

"A North Korean worker in our sewing factory."

"What?" She was so frightened. It took her a moment to find her voice again. "Is there anyone who knows about your relationship with her?"

"No one…"

"How long have you been seeing her?"

"I met her again in our sewing factory. I don't think it was a coincidence, more like my destiny!"

"*Again* in our factory?"

Pilsung nodded his head.

"It was my first day at work in Gaeseong. I couldn't see anybody but her among hundreds of workers. I didn't do it willingly. My steps automatically moved toward her and stopped in front of her. She also recognized me right away. I saw her hands shake so badly. She couldn't calm herself down. In an instant, the fingers of her right hand were accidentally squeezed between the moving parts of the sewing machine. I took her to the infirmary in a hurry. On the way to the infirmary, she repeated the same thing to me in a strong North Korean accent, on and on."

'I am delighted to see you again. I am so delighted... I knew that I would see you again.'

Yeook's cellphone rang loudly as she drove on the westbound Olympic Road along the bank of the Han River. She changed her radio to phone mode and answered.

"Hello?"

"Is this Yeook? I am an officer of the Seoul Metropolitan Police. Please stop by my office as soon as possible."

"What is this regarding?"

"I can't tell you on the phone."

The police officer hung up the phone. Yeook looked at Pilsung with a worrisome face. His face had already turned ashen in fear.

"You heard our conversation, right? Have the police already figured out your relationship with Soon? Is that why they're calling me? What do I do?"

"I don't know what to do. Please tell me what I can do, sister. If the police call me, I'll have to tell the truth."

She did not say anything at all. She drove up to the next exit, got off the Olympic Road, passed by downtown, and pulled into the parking lot of the Seoul Metropolitan Police. She walked into the building. Pilsung stayed at the parking lot and waited for her return. In an office of the police building, she found the police officer who had called her. He stood up out of his chair in a hurry as soon as he saw her.

"Thank you for stopping by. I couldn't tell you why you needed to come in over the phone because I honestly don't know why either. A military officer in an army installation on the front lines called me this morning. He asked me to locate and bring you to his office as soon as possible. He didn't say why he needs you, but I couldn't refuse his request. Shall we go?"

Yeook took out her cellphone from her handbag and called someone. They answered the phone on the first ring.

PILSUNG headed for a smoking section after Yeook entered the police building. A woman smoking there glanced at him. She was blowing cigarette smoke through her mouth with deep red lipstick. Red lipstick suddenly reminded him of Soon. Her lips always looked cherry-red without wearing lipstick. Pilsung recalled that day when the South Korean government made a decision on the shutdown of the Gaeseong Industrial Complex. He quietly called her out and took her to their secret place.

"I am so scared!" Soon said, her red lips turning blue.

"Take it easy. Don't worry, please."

"I have to worry!" Soon was so agitated. She bit her lip a bit too hard, leaving a bruise.

"I will visit North Korea and bring you out of there."

"Please don't joke like that." Her nerves also seemed to be on edge.

"I am not kidding. I am serious!" He grasped her hands with his own. They felt cold and wet.

"By all means, I will go and see you again, Pilsung! It doesn't matter to me where you are. Please don't forget my favorite poem and its last line. That's me."

"Soon, listen to me please. Escape to Yanbian, China, if all hopes have vanished in North Korea. I will see you there."

"Have you been in Yanbian?"

Pilsung shook his head. Soon didn't say anything afterword. Instead, she pressed him to her bosom and wrapped her arms around his waist with her fingers entwined. Her breath softly touched his earlobe for a moment. She raised her head and stared into his eyes. She kissed him on his lips and released her arms. Suddenly, she pushed him out of her arms and ran fast along the aisle inside the storehouse. Pilsung could not help but look at her while she ran to the end of the aisle.

The cellphone in his pocket rang loudly. It was Yeook calling him. He realized he had been caught up in the fantasy of Soon for a little while. He hurriedly answered the phone.

"Yes, sister!" he answered.

"..."

"All right. I understand." His phone conversation didn't last very long. Nevertheless, he seemed to have found peace of mind again.

A CAR stopped and waited for the right-turn signal at the crossroad before the bridge connected to Gangwha Island. The car made a right turn as soon as the light turned green and ran straight up to a Guard Post after about half an hour. An armed guard approached the car. He checked IDs and asked them to pull the car into the parking lot. Yeook and the police officer got out of the car. The guard guided them to the medical service unit. A uniformed medical officer warmly received the two visitors. The police officer introduced him to Yeook. The two seemed like they had known each other for a long time. The medical officer offered his hand to her.

"Do you know Soon Sul personally?"

"Soon?" She recalled Pilsung's words about Soon and realized it was finally happening. She had to stay cool and calm. She pretended to give it some thought. "Ah, she was a North Korean worker in my sewing factory."

"Yes, she was." He nodded his head, rose from his chair, and looked at Yeook, "This way, please."

He walked down along the aisle of the building and stopped walking in front of a door, at the end of the aisle. He unlocked and opened the door. Dead silence prevailed in the room. He walked a few steps further toward a bed. A white sheet seemed to be covering something. He turned his face and looked at Yeook.

"Please remove the white sheet."

Yeook removed the sheet carefully. *Oh, my god!* It was Soon's body lying on the bed.

"Soon? Why are you…?"

Yeook fell forward on the bed and fainted. When she woke up, she found herself lying down on a different bed getting an IV injection in her arm. The sunlight filtered through a small window crack. She covered her face with her hands. The medical officer was sitting on a chair next to the bed.

"I understand how deeply shocked you were by Soon's body. I am so sorry. She drowned while she was crossing the border river between South and North Korea. I have a question for you. Who is Pilsung?"

"…He is one of my staff," she answered very slowly.

"To my understanding, they were lovers."

He handed a plastic bag to her and said, "This was left to Pilsung by Soon."

Yeook respectfully received it with both hands. There was a handwritten memo to Pilsung in the plastic bag. She carefully pulled it out of the bag, but could hardly look at it. Her hand trembled so much that she couldn't hold it for reading.

THE POLICE officer drove back to Seoul with an expressionless face. Yeook wanted to hurry back to Seoul to rest in her office for a while. The medical officer didn't want to release the memo to Yeook at first, but she persistently persuaded him. Actually, it was more like she begged him to grant Soon's wish. She repeatedly said to him, "Soon crossed the river with a whole heart to see her lover again." He finally agreed under the condition that she would sign a security document. Yeook kept the memo in her handbag.

Yeook turned her head and looked out the car window. A boat was floating on the Han River. The wind made little waves on the surface of the water. The boat rolled lightly in the waves. She took several deep breaths, held her handbag with both hands, and took Soon's letter out of the handbag. She hesitated to open it for a little while and finally unfolded it with trembling hands. Soon's handwritten words came into Yeook's sight. Reading her handwriting made Yeook feel close to her. She could tell from the shape of the words that Soon was concerned and from others that she was determined. Some words were sad and others were almost hopeful. Yeook read it slowly.

'To my Pilsung,

I decided to cross the river to see you. If I get caught, I would rather throw myself into a strong current. Death would be better than life without you, Pilsung, because then I can be near you, day and night. I hope I cross the river safely. May we meet again, fate permitting. I love you, Pilsung.

From your Soon'

Yeook was sad beyond description. Her heart just bled for Soon. Tears dropped from her eyes while she read the letter. She couldn't stop crying for a while after she finished reading it. The police officer glimpsed her but she couldn't calm herself. She couldn't put the letter back in her handbag. Instead, she held it with both hands. Her cellphone rang, but she didn't answer.

She turned her face and looked outside again. The streets were packed with cars. People honked horns as they drove past. A car horn sounded like weeping. Yeook spoke to herself. "How did this sorrowful thing ever happen to me?" Soon's face rose in Yeook's mind. She felt afraid. She felt like a ghost was following her. The police officer drove his car in silence, keeping his eyes on the road ahead.

At twilight, Yeook finally returned and looked around her office. Pilsung seemed to make himself very busy in order to forget all his cares. All of a sudden, a feeling of hatred rose within her for him. She stared at him with anger and spoke to him in her mind. *Pilsung, don't you know that you are the reason for Soon's death? You know nothing about what happened to her. I would say that your love eventually led to her death. Life is so precious and should be worth more than anything else in the world.*

She walked around her office and after a moment, felt her anger ebb. She started to feel sorry for Pilsung. "You silly fool, Pilsung!" she mumbled to herself, looking at him, "How can I tell you about Soon? You will surely look for Soon if the Gaeseong Industrial Complex opens again. How can I tell you the story about Soon?"

Episode 2
A Shadow

HUMAN patience has its limits. Take it too far, and it destroys the mind. Pilsung obsessed over his memories with Soon and ached with longing for her. He experienced frequent hallucinations of Soon, such that people began to question his sanity. There were times he would rush into the street certain that he had seen her. Then he hurried to take a closer look. *Oh, no. It was not her!*

The situation was gradually deteriorating between the two Korean countries. Hopes for the reopening of the Gaeseong Industrial Complex were fading away as days and months passed. Pilsung couldn't wait any longer. Nobody could guarantee that Soon would come back to work at the sewing factory, even in the case of the reopening of the Industrial Complex.

After asking all around, he finally located a broker who would be able to smuggle him into North Korea. He made an appointment to meet the broker in Jamsil Subway Station. The broker preferred a busy place because he could quickly hide himself in the crowd if something unexpected happened to him. Pilsung and the broker sat face to face in a café.

"You need to disguise yourself as a Chinese merchant. That is the safest way to smuggle yourself into North Korea. You also need to prepare yourself for all eventualities." His plan for Pilsung was reasonable.

"What do you mean by all eventualities?"

"I mean… You may be eventually arrested by the Chinese police. In addition, North Korean secret agents may take…"

"I am ready for whatever comes and will do whatever you ask me to do," Pilsung interrupted the broker.

"You have to cross the Tumen River. It's very dangerous for you, but it's even more difficult for me. You may be shot to death if you get caught. Did you know that?"

"I really don't care. I need to make my way to North Korea. Also, I must locate a person before I get there. She is my reason for going."

"That's not difficult at all."

Pilsung handed a document on Soon to the broker. The broker carefully read it and nodded his head several times. He mumbled to himself, "Um… she is a girl of high standing in North Korea."

"Do you have her photos?" the broker carefully asked.

"I have some. Is it okay to release her photos to…?"

"North Korea is not a place where anyone can visit easily," he interrupted Pilsung's words, "It will be much easier to locate her if I have her photos."

Pilsung turned his head and looked outside. Many people were passing by. Some moved briskly and some moved slowly. A woman was looking around shopping areas. Pilsung thought that she resembled Soon very much. She was Soon. He suddenly stood up and rushed out the door, but he lost her in the crowd! He missed her and came back to his seat.

"Was there someone you knew?"

"I am very sorry. A woman walking around outside looked a lot like someone I know."

Pilsung began searching for her photos saved in his cellphone. Most of them were taken in their secret place of the sewing factory. He took pictures of her from many different angles, capturing every inch of her face. His eyes lit up on a photo of kissing her. The expression on her face looked a bit awkward but still so happy. He selected a picture to use for identification and sent it to the broker.

The broker left with Soon's photo, but Pilsung stayed alone at the café for a little while. He recalled the woman walking around outside the café. Yes, she was Soon, at least for him. She was a similar height to Soon. Her body, including her neckline, was very much like Soon's. Her walking style also resembled Soon's manner. She used to walk toward Pilsung with her chest sticking out just a bit, whenever she missed him. The woman outside the café walked like that. He began searching for her photos in his cellphone and found one striking a pose exactly like that.

Pilsung still had a clear memory of the day in March when the unusual spring snow was falling in large flakes. Most factory workers stopped working. They stared at the snow falling, mesmerized. Pilsung witnessed Soon standing up and walking toward the storehouse. He followed her with stealthy steps. She stopped walking in front of their secret place. Then she turned back abruptly, instead of pushing the door. Pilsung saw her chest sticking out just a bit. She ran into Pilsung's arms. They made love for the first time on that day. Doubt grew in Pilsung's mind. "She couldn't be Soon," Pilsung muttered to himself, shaking his head.

Why would she avoid me if she were Soon?

Pilsung glanced at his wristwatch. He supposed he would better be off leaving to meet them on time. He stood up out of his chair and walked away from the café. He looked around the shopping area again. Then he headed for Jamsil Subway Station and took the escalator down. He saw a woman hurriedly rushing down the stairs. He noticed right away that she was the woman who had stood outside the café a while ago. Pilsung followed her, but she had already boarded the train. He couldn't identify whether she was Soon or not.

He got off at Gangnam Station but couldn't walk forward. So many girls who resembled Soon were waiting for him. They walked toward and surrounded him. He was so confused. They drove him out of his senses. He couldn't tell who was who. All of them looked like Soon to him. He closed his eyes for a while. When he opened them, the girls were gone. He looked at his wristwatch. He was already late for his appointment. He rushed up the stairs.

BORA and Darim were waiting for someone in a coffee shop. Darim looked up at her watch, toying nervously with her camera on the table. *He should have been here 30 minutes ago.* Bora asked Darim to call him but Darim shook her head. What she wanted were facts and incidents for her newspaper story. The story would be very interesting if Bora's tips about him were true. She was strongly attracted to the love story between a South Korean man and a North Korean woman. It didn't matter how late he was, because he was a very important source. Such a story could break the ice and begin reconciling the tension between South and North Korea.

Darim looked at her watch again. Another ten minutes had passed. She felt she was getting impatient. *What if he never shows up?* Darim nervously looked at Bora and Bora picked up her phone to call him. At that instant, Pilsung rushed into the coffee shop. He looked so tired and weak. He sank down wearily into a chair.

"I heard that you have a girlfriend in North Korea. Is that true?" Darim asked him directly even before he sat down.

"A girlfriend in North Korea?" he looked unhappy with her question. He made a wry face. "That's impossible!" he fixed a keen stare on Darim.

"I heard your story from Bora." She turned her face to Bora, but Bora didn't say anything. She hardened her face when she heard Darim's words. She realized that she made a mistake. She didn't want to get him in trouble. Darim just told her that she was interested in the Gaeseong Industrial Complex.

"Darim, what I said…" Bora tried to stop the conversation, but Pilsung adamantly spoke first.

"I once said it just for fun to Bora. It was not my story at all. Hundreds of North Korean females worked in our sewing factory. It may be possible to have a love story between a man and a woman from South and North Korea. Right now I just worry about the future of our factory and the Gaeseong Industrial Complex."

"How long have you worked in Gaeseong?" Darim changed the topic of conversation.

"Three years. I started to work there as an intern…"

"As a journalist, I still remember that everybody hailed the Gaeseong Industrial Complex as an important step towards economic cooperation and reconciliation. I feel so sorry for the sudden halt there. I think that it was the last symbol of reunification for the two Koreas. Now, nothing shared remains between South and North Korea. We need good stories between the two Koreas if we're going to reestablish a positive relationship. It doesn't matter at an individual level, organizational level, or community level. That was the reason why I asked you to tell me the story about you and a woman in North Korea."

"Pilsung, you once told me that you met a North Korean woman in Gaeseong three years ago. I told Darim the story. Please don't misunderstand what I said to her," Bora had a concerned look. She needed to rationalize her actions sharing Pilsung's secret with Darim.

"I don't blame you, Bora. Don't worry," Pilsung looked at Darim and said, "Darim, I understand what you mean. My desire doesn't differ from yours. I, too, wish for the reopening of the Gaeseong Industrial Complex."

"I understand that you could have had a better job with your excellent academic career. What brought you to Gaeseong? I am so curious," Darim stared at Pilsung. He didn't tell anyone about Soon except for Yeook. How is it that Darim's questions so easily led to Soon? He had to evade her.

"That's a good question. The only thing I can say to you right now is, I had a dream. The dream brought me to Gaeseong. I still keep the dream in my mind. It is precious to me."

"What was his dream? Soon was his dream." He recalled Soon in his mind again. She always said she wanted to visit Seoul and walk along the streets with Pilsung. He wanted to grant her wish and once made a plan to secretly bring her to Seoul, disguising her as a part of merchandise. He carefully investigated customs clearance between South and North Korea. The process was not complicated, but rather simple. In addition, he noticed that customs officers sometimes didn't pay attention to merchandise in trucks. Pilsung told her about his plan; Soon turned down the plan immediately.

"I suppose you don't know about what's going on in North Korea. We have to ride a commuter bus at a given place and at a given time." Pilsung nodded his head. She continued, "State security agents always inspect the number of passengers on the bus, and do a full security scan twice a day, when we come to work and when we go home after work." She took a breath and continued with a tender voice, "I appreciate your time and efforts so much for making such a plan." She took a breath again and made a sad face. "What if they find I am not on the bus?'" She stood up slowly, bent, and kissed him on his cheek. He still felt her lips on his cheek from when she kissed him on that day.

"Please tell me your dream then," Darim intercepted his recall on Soon.
"...Pardon me?" Pilsung didn't hear because he was so focused on Soon.
"I asked what your dream was."
"Um...I can't tell you now. Maybe I will be able to tell you later when I have enough time and I'm ready for it, but not right now. I am sorry."
Pilsung wanted to discontinue his talking to Darim, although he didn't say it out loud. He was uncomfortable with her digging into the details of his situation. Darim also realized that she wouldn't get anything from him today. He was not ready for her interview at all. However, she fully sensed that he was guarding some interesting stories. She decided to collect secondary information about Pilsung from other sources. She excused herself from the table. Pilsung didn't say a word for a while. He had a few more sips of coffee. Bora spoke first.
"I am very sorry, Pilsung. I didn't mean to get you in trouble."
"Bora, you are my best friend. I know you didn't do it on purpose. I can't tell you right now. I am so exhausted mentally

and physically. Please don't say anything about me to anybody. I need your help. You are the only one who can help me. I will call you in a few days. I have to take care of something before I ask for your help. I will tell you further details later on."

"I am so sorry, Pilsung," Bora told him again.

She held his hands with hers. Pilsung looked at her. He saw tears beginning to well up in the corners of her eyes. He tapped her on the shoulder. At that instant, he had a strange feeling in his back. He turned around. The woman he saw in Jamsil Subway Station in the morning appeared again. He was dead sure. He didn't even say goodbye to Bora and rushed out of the coffee shop. Bora watched him until he went around the bend in the backstreets and left the scene.

"Pilsung was not himself," Bora muttered.

YEOOK was answering a phone in her office in the late afternoon. The person on the phone was the police officer who took her to the medical service unit in the army camp. He said that he would come over to her office. However, she didn't want a policeman to visit her office. It might have been her own prejudice, but she didn't have a good impression of the police. She told him she would stop by his office. He was pleased to oblige her.

"Pilsung seems to be too brave," he had a sip of coffee and looked at Yeook with wary eyes, "Is he going to visit China?"

"I think so. Is he under police surveillance?"

"Just to be sure. He has to behave himself."

"I don't understand what you mean."

"Have you thought about the ramifications if his story about the North Korean woman found dead was published in the newspaper?"

"My goodness! Who knows the story? And who is writing it and what newspaper?"

"Not yet. However, I obtained a piece of intelligence. A journalist who works for a prestigious newspaper is beginning an investigation," he spoke in a voice filled with conviction.

His phone rang in the middle of the conversation with Yeook. He excused himself to answer his phone. He walked out of his office and entered a small seminar room next to his office. There was a window between the two rooms. Yeook could see him talking on the phone to someone.

The police officer seemed to listen very carefully.

"It was just my guess. That was true," he said.

He nodded and seemed to comfort the person on the phone.

"I understand your situation very well. You'll still have to wait a few months. However, it will not take long."

While the person on the phone talked to him, he was smiling and leaning on the table next to him.

"Please don't go outside frequently. You shouldn't be caught. Please hide yourself in a safe place," he ended the call and came back to his office. Yeook asked him as soon as he sat on his chair.

"A journalist? Is he or she digging into Pilsung's private affairs?" Yeook looked serious.

"Ask Pilsung. He knows. Please ask him to behave himself. That's all I can say at this point."

"What do you think will happen if I hand Soon's memo to Pilsung? I think we need to make him give up on Soon."

"What are you talking about? My answer is absolutely no. You shouldn't release the memo to him yet. I have to do some paper work for her because she was found to be a dead person in South Korea. Please wait until I finish my paper work."

Yeook trudged with heavy feet on her way back. She didn't know what to do about the situation. She took out her cellphone from her handbag and called Pilsung.

BACKSTREETS are a thing for which Seoul is famous, although they are ravaged by decadence to a certain degree. It is to the backstreets that people in Seoul always flock for fun at the end of the day. They meet their friends and lovers. They sometimes come across old friends they haven't seen for a long time.

On that day, Pilsung became one of the people on the backstreets. Yeook invited him to dinner and drinks. He looked around and found the restaurant right away that she told him about on the phone. He pushed the door and entered the restaurant. He found her already having a drink alone.

"Pilsung, forget about Soon and date another girl. Don't you know that there are many fish in the ocean?" she said. Her first words were so blunt. Pilsung didn't say a word but looked at her. She filled his cup with rice wine, which is called *makgeolli*.

"Well, as a matter of fact, I have…a note…"

Yeook stopped talking to him. She did not have the heart to tell the truth to him, having a face-to-face conversation. Instead, she opened and put her hand in her handbag. She held the memo and took out her hand; however, her hand was empty. She closed her bag carefully.

"Empty your cup, Pilsung."

Yeook held up her cup and Pilsung followed her. They clinked their cups together. They drained their cups in one gulp for different reasons.

"Do you miss Soon that much?" she said and stared at him. He looked so pathetic.

"I don't know why. I have seen some girls who look like Soon on the street. I saw them here and there," Pilsung finally brought up his words.

"Forget about her. The pursuit of love, it's all futile!" she said and stretched out her arm to the handbag again. She opened and put her hand into the bag. The memo, covered with a plastic bag, was still there but she couldn't pull it out. She closed her bag again.

"Cheers!"

Yeook raised her cup. Pilsung did, too. They emptied their cups again. Pilsung filled her cup first and his later.

"I admire a romantic like you, Pilsung," Yeook said.

"A romantic?" Pilsung laughed loudly. Then he searched for Soon's photos in his cellphone and handed it to her. "Sister, please look at Soon's photos. She looks so pretty, doesn't she?"

Yeook turned over photos, saved in the phone, one by one with her finger. The two were a perfect match. Yeook couldn't say a word about Soon's will to Pilsung. They left the restaurant and walked staggering together along the backstreets.

After a while, Pilsung sensed someone following him. He stopped walking and he looked back and watched as Soon walked away fast. All of sudden, he felt sobered up. He rubbed his eyes. Certainly, she was Soon! He grabbed a hold of Yeook's arm.

"What's wrong, Pilsung?"

"Sister, look… look at her over there!"

Her eyes followed his finger pointing at a woman. Soon was standing over there!

"Is she… Soon?"

Her eyes bulged at the sight of Soon. Her steps were frozen to the spot. Soon is dead and not of this world.

"Soon!"

Pilsung was shouting her name and running to her Yeook also shouted to Pilsung.

"No, Pilsung! She is not Soon. She shouldn't be Soon!"

Episode 3
A Tailing

YEOOK remained awake all night. She couldn't free herself from what she saw. The girl surely resembled Soon. *No!* She *was* Soon. Yeook was so confused. Certainly, Soon was lying on the bed covered with a white sheet in a chill room. *Then, who was the woman on the backstreet last night?* A dead woman cannot stride on the street. *A ghost then?* She shook her head. At dawn, she finally dropped off to sleep for a little while.

Yeook saw Soon in her dreams. Soon pawed the air to get out of a deep, gray swamp. Yeook asked her why she was trapped there. Soon didn't answer her question. Instead, she reached out her hand to Yeook. She asked if Yeook would take her hand. Yeook reached out in reply. Then, Soon flew like a bird and softly landed in front of Yeook.

"Caw, Caw, Caw!" Crows raised their heads, flew in the sky, and began to sing loudly. They aroused Yeook from a deep sleep in the early morning. She opened her eyes, but the illusion of Soon would not disappear. Certainly, she was Soon. No, she couldn't be! She shook her head again. She went to her office first thing in the morning and called the police officer.

"Thank you for calling, Yeook," he warmly received her on the phone.

"I saw Soon on the street last night."

"Soon? Your employee in Gaeseong? You said you saw her? How? That's not possible! You are the person who identified her body on the bed in the chill room."

"Well, I shouldn't say this, but I have to. Are there any conspiracies to cover up Soon's case? I really don't understand what happened last night."

"…Um… I don't know what you are talking about. Where was she? Did she say that she is Soon? What else did she say to you?" he hesitated for a while, waiting for her response.

"She just ran away from us. Pilsung and I couldn't catch her. I didn't have a chance to talk to her. I mean, she resembled Soon so much."

"You see? Now you told me she resembled Soon. If she were Soon, she would have had no reason to avoid you or Pilsung."

Pilsung accidently overheard Yeook talking to someone on the phone. Her door stood half open. She seemed to be talking about Soon. He walked near the door but couldn't hear her conversation clearly. However, he could clearly recognize that she was frequently mentioning Soon. He wondered who was on the phone and about their conversation. Pilsung could easily guess that Yeook must have shared something on Soon with the person on the phone.

Last night, Pilsung ran all over the backstreets looking for Soon but couldn't find her. All his efforts ended in vain. When he came back to Yeook, she was still standing up at the same spot. He said to Yeook, "She was Soon for sure." Her reply was quite unexpected.

She said to him, "She was a ghost of Soon to me." She looked very serious. She seemed to be so scared. She was quaking with fear. He had to take her home. It was well past one o'clock in the morning when he came back home.

Yeook talked long on the phone. He tried to eavesdrop on her conversation outside the door. There was not much valuable information in the conversation. He simply thought that her conversation on the phone was quite cathartic. She needed such a conversation for a release of shock from last night. They seemed to talk about a memo seriously. Pilsung knocked on the door as soon as she hung up the phone.

"Come in, Pilsung."

BORA felt sorry for Pilsung. She surely got him in trouble a few days ago. His voice still echoed in her mind. '*I am so exhausted mentally and physically.*' He seemed to be going out of his mind. She didn't want to blame anybody but she felt betrayed by Darim. Bora punched Pilsung's number into her cellphone.

"Pilsung, I am so sorry. Would you forgive me, please?"

"Don't worry, Bora. Your apology has been already accepted. By the way, you have to promise me just one thing."

"I promise. What is it?"

"Don't say anything about what I am doing to anybody."

"I won't. I promise."

"Would you do me a favor? You are the only one who can do it for me now."

"I will. Tell me what."

"I can't say it over the phone."

"How come?"

Pilsung was not his usual self. He loved sitting in a café and chatting with his friends. That was himself but today he didn't want to meet with Bora in a closed space like a café or restaurant. He usually gave a straightforward answer but today he avoided a straightforward answer to her question. Bora asked him on the phone several times about what he wanted her to do. But his answer was, "No, not on the phone."

Bora arrived at the spot where Pilsung indicated – a restaurant. She was preoccupied watching people move in and out of the restaurant, when someone grabbed her arm from behind. It was Pilsung.

"You frightened me!" she looked back and said.

"Shall we walk?" He walked along the backstreets where he saw Soon the other night. He stopped at the spot where he saw Soon or a shadow of Soon and turned his face to Bora. He looked around carefully and said to her.

"Bora, I want you to tap a wireless phone for me."

"What? Are you crazy?"

"Bora, I am not crazy. I am serious." Pilsung looked serious. He nodded his head as if he forced her to say yes.

"It's illegal! Do you want me to commit a crime?"

"Of course, it is illegal. That's why I am asking you now. I also trust you that you would get away without a trace."

"I have done it countless times with my friends. But we didn't do it for fun! We were polishing our hacking skills. I also haven't done it without permission from the authorities."

"Bora, I am not asking you to do it for fun. This is a matter of life and death. I can save someone's life if I do this at the right time in a proper way. I need to know what they are saying on the phone. I need it terribly. Please don't refuse my request."

"Okay, Pilsung, but I can't do it by myself. I will have to do it with my colleagues; I mean, I would need several hackers if I decide to do it. I will have to locate them because I haven't been in touch with them for quite some time. Please give me a list of names and their phone numbers. I will check first and let you know. I can only do it a couple of times though. Please remember our saying, '*The pitcher goes to the well so often that it is broken at last.*'"

'Bora and Guys' was once a famous group of hackers, although it was dissolved many years ago. Pilsung was not a regular member, but he got along with them frequently. Bora was a leader but not the best in her members. Chulbang and Sooil were the best. They also had good connections with other hackers, including members of 'Anonymous International'.

Chulbang is now operating a dream-making business. *Making a dream for someone else? Is that possible?* Bora once asked him to explain but she still doesn't know exactly what he means. According to him, our brain usually makes dreams through the mind. He has a smart phone app for dream-making. He and a psychologist invented it. We must have a story in our dream ahead of time for it to work. His dream-making app helps the story activate in our brain by hacking the mind while its owner is talking on the phone, watching videos or TV, or listening to music. He's been making dreams for his customers for years. His business is in good shape, according to him.

Sooil runs a security business as a cyber-policeman. He created it himself. He is not an official government employee but frequently works for government authorities, especially the police. He is proud of himself as a watchdog of cyberspace. His nickname is Bundol, or lightning bolt. He used his nickname while he was a member of Bora and Guys. Bora, after thinking for a while, decided to meet with Sooil first because he is more serious than Chulbang. Bora punched Sooil's number into her cellphone.

"Bora, long time no see!"

"I need your help, Sooil."

"You know what? Chulbang is here with me!" he seemed excited. As far as Bora knew, the two were very close friends. Whenever they got together, they created something interesting. Now they must be up to something new. They had come up with a dream-making project and a cyber-watchdog project last time they met and brainstormed. Bora wondered what would come of this meeting.

"What a coincidence! I was about to call him, too."

"Have you dreamed recently?"

"Yes, I have."

"Chulbang told me that he had made and secretly sent a wonderful dream to you. I like to know whether you had this dream."

"He did? What an interesting story! Tell me about the dream."

"Come over to my office and check if his dream-hacking job has effectively worked for you or not."

A CAR drove out of the Seoul Metropolitan Police building. Pilsung followed the car in a taxi. The car ahead passed Gwanghwamoon Plaza, ran through downtown Seoul, and stopped at the parking lot of the National Medical Center. The police officer, an acquaintance of Yeook, got out of the car and entered the hospital. Pilsung got out of the taxi and walked carefully after him. The police officer went up in the elevator and entered a hospital room. Pilsung passed by the room and carefully observed its nametag.

"Chulyoung Lee?"

Immediately after Pilsung passed by, the door opened. Pilsung hid himself around the corner of a corridor. The police officer went down in the elevator and crossed the street as soon as the light changed to green. He headed for a restaurant in the backstreets.

Pilsung watched the police officer enter the restaurant one block away from the place. He waited for a few minutes, then entered the restaurant, too. He cautiously looked around the hall.

The restaurant was very crowded. Pilsung pretended to look for his friends, all the while paying close attention to the police officer. He sat several tables away from the police officer and ordered a bottle of beer with a dish of Korean sausage or s*oondae*. The police officer was surrounded by a group of students at the table. He shook hands with them one by one.

"What grade are you in, Sangbok?"

"I am a junior in high school," Sangbok answered.

"Three years have passed since you first arrived in Seoul," the police officer said.

"Sangbok and his sister, and Moohwan's three family members arrived in Seoul today three years ago. So, today is their 'other' birthday. I am here to celebrate."

"Thank you very much, sir!"

"Don't mention it. It is my pleasure to hold your hands. Ah, I visited Chulyoung just before I came here. He is getting better."

The police officer seemed to support North Korean defectors. The North Korean defectors reminded Pilsung of Soon. He saw a waiter deliver a birthday cake to their table. *When was Soon's birthday? It was April 4th.* Pilsung gave her the nickname *Sawol* or April in English. She loved her nickname. Pilsung had a pair of matching promise rings prepared for her first birthday since their meeting. He held the box in his pocket all day long on that day, but couldn't catch a chance to put the ring on her finger. Whenever he peeped through the window into the sewing room where Soon was working, he found her focused on her work. She didn't even raise her head.

By the late afternoon Pilsung could wait no longer. He finally decided to stop by her sewing room and pass a memo to her. Pilsung waited for Soon in the corner of the storehouse full of clothing boxes until she showed up herself. Eventually, he heard the sound of footsteps outside. It was about 30 minutes prior to the official closing time. Soon stopped walking in front of him. He spoke to her, "Please show me your left hand, Soon." She extended her hand and looked at him curiously. Pilsung hurriedly slipped the ring on her fourth finger, "Happy birthday to you, Soon."

"What a beautiful birthday gift it is. You are so sweet, Pilsung."

Then Pilsung handed the other ring to Soon asking her to put it on his finger. Soon did not hesitate to do that. She looked at him for a second and gave him a big hug. Soon especially loved the pattern of orchid flowers on the rings. An orchid flower is a symbol of nobility. The ring looked pretty on her finger. Soon asked Pilsung to take a picture of their ringed fingers. In another moment, she asked Pilsung to slip the ring off her finger. Pilsung still remembers the moment when she asked him to do that. He felt so disappointed and hesitated to comply.

"Don't worry, Pilsung. I have already accepted your offer. We will lose everything whenever they notice I have a relationship with you. Please keep it well until we have a safe place to store it."

It was on that day when Pilsung decided to make a secret place just for the two of them. He spoke to Soon, "April is one of the most beautiful months. I wish I could bring and show you spring in Seoul."

She responded, "I wish I could walk hand in hand with you on the streets in Seoul. When will that day arrive in front us?" Soon left the storehouse first, and Pilsung stayed there for a little while. He watched her retreating figure. From the back, Soon looked so lonely on that day.

The police officer abruptly stood up answering his phone and moved toward the restroom. Pilsung sensed the cellphone in his pocket vibrating. He answered the phone and immediately rose from his chair. He paid with cash and rushed out of the restaurant. The police officer in front of the restroom suddenly raised his voice on the phone.

"What? What did you say?"

He turned his face and looked around the restaurant for a moment. Pilsung quickly hid himself behind a building and hurried into passengers on the street. He walked straight without looking back.

A woman walked on the tail of Pilsung. She was tall and had a nice figure. She stopped when Pilsung stopped. She moved forward when Pilsung did. Pilsung went down to the subway entrance and so did she.

BORA stayed around 50 to 100 meters behind Pilsung. He dialed a code number as soon as Sooil sent her a signal. In his office, Sooil confirmed Bora's cellphone was ready for eavesdropping on phone conversations with the police officer on his monitor. When the police officer answered his cellphone, Bora could hear the conversations without interfering with the phone call at all.

"I told you that you can come over tonight. Why didn't you show up?"

"I was on my way. I saw a man follow you around the restaurant. I stopped walking because I was afraid of being caught by him."

"Was I followed by a man? Where is he now?"

"He entered the restaurant, must be somewhere in the hall."

Bora was frightened by the phone conversation and made an emergency call to Pilsung.

"Hey, Pilsung, leave the restaurant immediately and hide yourself as soon as possible. You are being followed by a woman, too," she said.

Bora saw the police officer talking on the phone walk out of the restaurant after Pilsung hid himself behind the building. Bora looked around the street, the woman walking behind

Pilsung had already gone. However, she could hear their conversations.

"You still speak with a strong North Korean accent."

"I am trying to use a Seoul accent."

"Can you describe the stranger who followed me?"

"Well, I couldn't see his face, but his back only... Um... He looked young."

"What else could you see about him?"

"Ah, he was tall and slim. I think he must be a nice-looking guy."

"I am glad you've recovered your sense of humor."

Their call ended. Sooil removed all traces of the wiretap. He double checked every connection. Bora left the spot right after she received a message from Sooil.

"Everything clear."

"All right. You are the man, Bundol," Bora sent the same message to him by text.

PILSUNG recalled the broker's words again. The busiest place is the safest one. He took the subway and let Bora know where he was heading. Just to be sure, he got out of his cabin of the train at Konkuk University Station, looked around carefully, and quickly got into the next cabin just before the train door closed.

The woman who followed Pilsung around the restaurant was staying in a far corner of the cabin with her back turned, only occasionally casting a side glance in his direction. She saw him get out of his cabin. She approached the door and observed his moves very carefully from her position.

She moved her steps toward the next cabin right after the train left the station. Pilsung stood next to the door holding a strap with his right hand. He got off at Gangnam Station. She left the station and carefully followed him again. Pilsung stopped walking in front of a café and looked around. He found Bora waiting for him. He carefully moved toward her and grabbed her arms.

"You frightened me, Pilsung!" She turned around to face him.

"Who did the police officer speak with on the phone?"
"I don't know her name."
"Did she speak with a North Korean accent?"
"Yes, she did. Her sentences ended with 'neda' instead of 'nida', and 'siyo' instead of 'seyo'," Bora impersonated her speech several times and laughed loudly.
"Did they mention Soon at all in their conversations?"
"I guess the woman on the phone seems to be a new arrival. Is she Soon?"
"That's not possible. She should come and see me first, if she is in Seoul. It's me! I am the reason for her visit to Seoul. She has no reason to hide herself from me!" he said firmly.

So he said but he couldn't cast away his doubt on the woman equivalent to Soon on the backstreet the other day. *Who was she?* Yeook had also agreed she looked like Soon. When he asked about her pervious conversation with someone on the phone about Soon, Yeook just said, "I called to report the sighting to the police." She didn't hesitate at all.

Pilsung knew the regulation. Yeook was obligated to report to the police on her North Korean workers. She should have done it if one of her workers was in Seoul. Pilsung searched for everything around the police officer, instead of directly calling him and asking questions. He spent his time on this investigation with Bora, but he couldn't find any clues on Soon. "What shall I do?" he talked to himself with soundlessness. "What shall I do?" he repeated.

"Wake up, Pilsung!"

Bora tapped him on his shoulder and linked her arm in his. Pilsung turned to her, smiling. He felt comfortable with Bora and could snap himself out of his funk for a while. On that particular day, the two looked especially happy together.

"Pilsung, you must be hungry. Let's go to have a nice dinner. I will treat you tonight."

Bora turned around and looked at Pilsung's profile carefully. His face in the profile was exactly the same as what she had seen in her dream. The dream was so vivid that she could remember all the details in it. She was surrounded by a group of men and women. They closed in around her, trying to deprive her of the precious thing in her hand. A girl in the circle stepped forward and said, "Give it to me, and you will be safe." Bora refused it. The group then broke into choruses of 'give it to her' several times. Bora then squatted on her haunches. They grabbed her and forcefully tried to open her hand. In that moment, a guy burst onto the circle. He lifted her up in his arms and glared at them. Then all the men and women disappeared. The guy was Pilsung.

"You know what? You were my hero in my dream," Bora softly held Pilsung's arm with her hands.

"Really? Have you dreamed of me? Did I behave myself in your dream? Tell me about it," Pilsung looked at Bora with a big smile.

"Actually, Chulbang made and sent it to me. Can you imagine? I had his story in my dream. I mean that his story has been actualized in my dream. He is a dream-hacker indeed."

"I heard that his business is in good shape now."

"Yes, it is. He seems to be satisfied with what he is doing now."

"He has made a variety of dreaming modules. My dream must be one of them."

Pilsung was absorbed in the conversation with Bora. He didn't realize that a woman had followed him. The woman walking behind Pilsung stopped when Pilsung stopped. She walked when Pilsung walked. She also saw Pilsung with his eyes on a girl as she secretly approached them. The girl had a beautiful smile and looked so happy with Pilsung. They looked like a couple in love indeed.

The woman, still far away from them, stumbled slightly as if she was out of step. She slowed her pace and stopped completely as if she had lost her motivation to follow Pilsung. She held her head in both hands and thought for a moment. She bent her back to sit on the bare ground and immediately staggered back to her feet. She stared at Pilsung for a moment, straightening her back. She then moved a couple of steps back, turned around, and left with heavy steps. She walked fast and ran along the backstreets. Tears welled up in her eyes.

Episode 4
A Rhapsody of the Tumen River

HANA drove her car on her way to the airport after having a late breakfast. As usual, she felt a sort of excitement when meeting a new customer. She enjoyed meeting new people and therefore took this side job a couple of years ago. Her official job was monotonous and boring. She couldn't stand it and looked for a side job related to what she had done for a living. She didn't do it for money, just for fun.

She looked forward to meeting him today. Her partner in Seoul asked her to escort him around every corner of the Yanbian area. He must be a special one. *Is he a nice-looking guy?* She heard that he was looking for a girl. He will be able to find her, if he is lucky. It won't be easy, though. He will probably get into danger, because the streets in Yanbian are thronged with secret agents from South Korea, North Korea and China. She has to protect him. She received a picture of the girl a couple of days ago. *Who is she?* A phone call cut off her imagination.

"Hello?" she answered.

The person on the cellphone was her boss from her official job.

"Did you say that his name is Pilsung?"

"Yes, sir. I understand!"

She mused to herself right after she put the phone down. *What a coincidence! He is a man on my boss's list in Seoul. I have to meet his demands. Fine! He is also a customer. I have to meet his requests, too. No problem! How interesting!* She pulled her car in the parking lot and entered the arrival hall.

Pilsung had no choice but to visit North Korea. No hope remained to see Soon in Gaeseong or in Seoul. Right after South Korea declared the permanent shutdown of the Gaeseong Industrial Complex, he boarded a plane for Tumen in China with the broker's help. The broker has already made various arrangements for him in Tumen. His airplane landed at Yanji International Airport. He went through the entry procedure and made his way toward the arrival gate. He walked out of the gate and looked around for a minute. He saw an elegant and intelligent looking woman approaching him.

"Are you Pilsung Nam?" she said.

"Yes, I am."

"I had a phone call from Seoul. I will be your guide while you stay in China."

Pilsung put his luggage in the trunk and sat in the passenger seat. She spread a map of Yanbian on the dashboard and looked at Pilsung.

"We are here in Yanji and will drive up to Tumen. It will take about an hour with no traffic."

She marked a long and wiggly green line from Yanji through Tumen with a highlighter pen. The green line ended at the northernmost point on the Korean peninsula. He was scheduled to cross the Tumen River to be smuggled into North Korea.

The broker told him that a third man will approach and guide him to cross the river toward North Korea. At this point, Pilsung won't know anything about him at all. The broker will let him know about him a week later. Meanwhile, Pilsung decided to look for any trace of Soon in Yanbian. He took out his notebook from his sack and opened. He wrote down every detail of her in his notebook. The car passed through the tollgate.

"This is the highway from Yanji through Tumen. We say 'Domoon', but the Chinese call this place 'Tumen'," she said.

"May I ask your name?"

"Ah, I am sorry. I am Hana, Hana Kim."

THE POLICE officer sat in his chair without saying a word. He turned his head to the window and made a serious face. Yeook opened her handbag and pulled out Soon's will wrapped with a plastic bag. She pushed it to the police officer sitting on her opposite side.

"I have no reason to keep this memo in my bag. I should have given it to Pilsung," she broke the silence between them.

He didn't say anything and alternated looking at the memo and at her. He again looked out the window. The silence continued between them.

"You should have let me release this damn memo to Pilsung. Then he wouldn't have even thought about visiting Yanbian."

"It's my fault but I still can't give you permission. I have just one thing that I didn't tell you. I shouldn't at this point. It's almost ready now. Please take it back," he pushed the memo to Yeook.

"Maybe, he is already in North Korea."

"Not easy at all."

"I will go to Yanji and bring him back to Seoul," Yeook brought Bora to mind. She met Bora several years ago through Pilsung. At that time, Bora was a media arts professional helping her promote her sewing products around the world through smartphone apps. She did her job very well. She was a stylish girl who looked gorgeous even if she wore a sack. She requested Yeook to visit the sewing factory in Gaeseong. Yeook asked Pilsung to take her on a tour of her factory.

Yeook asked about Bora's feelings at the factory after she returned from her tour. Bora said, "I feel pity for North Korean workers in the Industrial Complex. My mom used to tell me that she worked in a wig factory."

Yeook asked again, "Did she?"

Bora continued, "Yes, she did. I could see my mom among the factory workers in Gaeseong. My mom had started working as a factory girl right after she graduated from high school. I was told that she would work 16 hours a day, seven days a week. She couldn't even think about days off."

Bora's words, 'please treat them well', still remained in Yeook's mind. Yeook thought that Pilsung and Bora would make a great pair. One day Yeook asked her if she ever loved Pilsung. She answered that she loved him but as a friend. Bora may know where Pilsung is staying in Yanbian. Yeook looked at the police officer as if asking for his consent for her to fly to Yanbian.

"No, you won't. I will locate him first and let him come back to Seoul. Please, wait for several days." His position on the issue was firm.

"How will you do that?"

"I'm a police officer. I have my methods."

He didn't give her a specific answer and stood up from his chair. He didn't even turn his eyes on Soon's memo. Instead, he extended his hand to her. Yeook held his hand with her right hand and picked up Soon's memo on the table with her left. She handed it to him, but he wouldn't even look at it. He stopped in front of the door and looked back at her.

"I met Pilsung a couple of days ago. I told him to stop by my office but he hasn't yet. I am almost ready to let him know the full story. Don't worry. He is already in my reach. It doesn't matter where he is."

"You said, you met Pilsung? Why didn't you tell me about it?"

"He is a nice young man," he looked back at Yeook but avoided her question.

He walked out the door and Yeook sat back on her chair. She touched Bora's number on her cellphone. She didn't answer the phone. Bora called her back after a while. Yeook asked the name and location of Pilsung's lodging. She didn't know either. She didn't have enough information on Pilsung's whereabouts in Yanbian.

"Isn't there any way I can contact Pilsung? As you know, it's urgent."

"…Um, I can possibly use the location tracking to locate Pilsung but it would take some time. I will send him a text message for you."

PILSUNG didn't sleep well last night from the tingle of excitement. The sound of a train whistle was nostalgic in his mind. He was born and raised nearby a small train station. His siblings disliked the train whistle but he had always liked it. To him, sometimes it sounded like music and sometimes whisperings between passengers in the train. He drew a variety of images from the train whistle last night, as he had done when he was a child.

One day he said to Soon, "I will show you a secret place just for us."

Soon opened her eyes wide, "A secret place for us? What exciting news this is!" She was delighted. He led her to a small space made of partitioned walls in the corner of the storehouse full of cloth boxes. From the outside, the space didn't look like a room at all, but a stack of boxes with clothes inside. He put a pair of chairs in the room, one for Soon and another for himself. It was a small but comfortable place for them to let their love grow. They had their first kiss in the room that day.

Early in the morning, he left his hotel and walked along the bank of the Tumen River. He heard a train whistle again. A host of happy memories with Soon were pressing in on him. Momentarily, he was under the delusion that he walked hand in hand with Soon. Her hands were soft and warm. He could even feel the ring on her finger. Pilsung always wore the promise ring on his finger. He also carried Soon's ring around his neck. He then felt her day and night. He would put the ring on her finger the moment he finds her. The train passed by, but he could hardly see it. A heavy layer of fog covered the river. A few steps ahead, two women conversed,

"I saw a North Korean boy being dragged by a Chinese policeman."

"When?"

"Ah, just yesterday!"

"What happened?"

"The policeman was a cold-hearted guy! The boy cried and begged for mercy…" she stopped talking for a minute and blew her nose loudly, "A crowd of onlookers gathered at the scene. All of them held their breath and looked at them."

"Did the policeman hand the poor child over to North Korea?"

"Yes, he did. He forcefully dragged the boy to the China-North Korea Bridge. The boy was treated like a dog. He couldn't even cry. His pants got all wet with piss."

"What a beast! What if North Korea would be better off?" she clicked her tongue.

"You know what? The boy stopped crying and stood at attention in front of North Korean guards. Yes, he sure did."

Pilsung stopped walking and looked back. A wave of fear swept over him. The boy could be Soon. *What if she had already been dragged out by the North Korean secret police?* He looked all the way around the riverbank. Nothing could be clearly seen. The fear he felt was literally breathtaking. He stopped walking for a while. The fog had slightly cleared. Then, he calmed down a bit. The Tumen River Hotel was within his sight. He could recognize North Korean soldiers moving in the trenches across the Tumen River. He also could see the bridge where a North Korean boy was taken away like a dog.

HANA arrived at the Tumen River Hotel just on time. She waited for him for ten minutes in the lobby, but Pilsung did not show up. She called him in his guest room, but he didn't answer the phone. She went up to his room and knocked on the door. He was not there. She left the hotel to look for Pilsung.

A Chinese policeman in plain clothes in the lobby watched Hana's movements carefully. He moved toward the front desk and asked some questions to a man sitting there. He came back to his place and called someone somewhere. He spoke so quietly in Chinese that nobody recognized what he said.

Hana went up the stairs and stopped on the bank of the Tumen River. She observed closely the area around the riverbank. Pilsung was nowhere to be seen. She started walking toward the China-North Korea Bridge. Her cellphone rang. She moved faster while talking on the phone,

"I understand."

She didn't talk but listened to someone on the phone. She hung up the phone and moved toward downtown Tumen. The streets were quiet. She could see only a few people passing by. She stopped and turned the direction of the riverbank.

Her phone rang again. She answered and just listened. The words she did speak were yes or no. She became obsessed with looking for Pilsung. Again, she stood up on the bank of the Tumen River. She went toward the Tumen River Hotel.

"All right, sir. I will take care of him very carefully."

She said this and turned off her cellphone completely. She didn't want her cellphone ringing to bother her while she looked for Pilsung. He could be in trouble. All kinds of dark thoughts passed through her mind. Her steps quickened.

PILSUNG found several men fishing at the riverside of the Tumen River. He carefully went down to the riverside and stepped toward an old man. He looked like he was in his seventies and had a lot of winkles on his face and neck.

"Hello, sir! Any luck this morning?" He looked like a Korean, therefore he spoke to him in Korean.

"The current is so swift. So, no luck yet! Where are you from?" the old man had a strong North Korean accent.

"I am from Seoul."

"Did you come here for business?"

"I am going to visit Jungam Village. I am looking for a woman."

"I am from Jungam Village."

"Really?"

"Are you still living there?"

"I live in Tumen now."

"The Suls are still living there?"

"The Suls?" He thought for a moment, "Ah, they left Jungam Village a long time ago as far as I know."

Pilsung wanted to ask questions about the Suls, but he hesitated to talk about the family and Jungam Village any more. Pilsung finally came into Hana's sight. She stepped down and hurried over to him. In that instant, Pilsung could hear fast footsteps.

"You are here! Jesus, you scared me this morning! I have been looking for you for an hour!"

"You must be a henpecked husband. Please go ahead," the old man said.

The old man got ready for leaving the spot. Pilsung came back to the hotel with Hana.

HANA drove her car for around an hour, but she did not speak a word. Pilsung sat in the passenger seat. She crossed over a brook and pulled out into an unpaved road. Finally, a road sign for Jungam Village came into her sight. Hana opened her mouth,

"I think you are too trusting. Don't trust people here in China. You could get in trouble!"

"…He told me he is from Jungam Village."

Jungam Village (亭岩村) was established by a group of Koreans in 1938 in the Japanese colonial era. A group of some 80 families in Chungcheongdo had to leave their home villages according to the forced migration policy of the Japanese governor in Korea. They named their village Jungam after they arrived at this place, surrounded by a long walled mountain fortress. The fortress was built by Koreans in the era of Goguryeo (38 B. C. – 668 A. D.).

The village people still kept their Korean traditions alive. Several elderly persons in the village still spoke in Chungcheong dialect although they came to this place with their parents in their childhood. They still liked to sing the song 'Chungju Arirang' when they would celebrate something memorable. Arirang is one of the most popular Korean folk songs inscribed on the Representative List of the Intangible Cultural Heritage of Humanity program by UNESCO. More than 3,000 versions of Arirang have been handed down by tradition in Korea. This Chungju Arirang has already disappeared in Korea, but remains alive in such a small village of Koreans in Tumen, China. Thatched-roof houses are still there, although they are rare even in the countryside in Korea.

Hana and Pilsung entered the Village Hall. A group of five older persons sat and chatted with others. Pilsung bowed low to them, and asked,

"His last name was Sul, but I don't know his name. Do you recognize the Sul family?"

"Did you say Mr. Sul? I moved to this village when I was five years old. My parents always longed for their home village in Korea. The Sul family was very close to my parents. They moved to North Korea but frequently came to see us before 2000. They stopped visiting about ten years ago."

"Don't you remember? A granddaughter of Mr. Sul came to visit us a couple of years ago," an older person sitting next to Hana intervened in the conversation.

"You are right! She told us that she came here crossing the China-North Korea Bridge. It was on her way to working in Tumen. She said she would come back, but she never showed up again."

Pilsung thought to himself in silence, *She must be Soon.* He could feel his heart start to pound and his face turned red. She pulled out his cellphone and to show them her photos. They nodded their heads, but they didn't look one hundred percent certain.

"She was here, right?"

"Yes, she was. North Koreans came to work at Tumen by crossing the Tumen River Bridge. She didn't say where exactly. She just mentioned a factory."

"Do you have any ideas what kind of factory it was? Maybe a clothing factory or a sewing factory?" Pilsung asked hurriedly.

"I sure don't know. She didn't even sit down. A North Korean guard was looking at her. She just said, she was here to say hello to us and continued on her way. I don't know exactly, but I can guess she paid lots of money to the guard for visiting us."

"Please let me know what else she said to you."

"Um… Well…"

The old man carefully studied Hana's face. Hana left the scene for a while, but none in the Village Hall said any more to Pilsung. Some time elapsed before an old man spoke to Pilsung, after Hana left.

"Have you heard North Korea's Special Economic Zone in between Yanji and Tumen? Its official name is the Tumen Special Economic Zone."

"Yes, I have. I was told that the Economic Zone is almost shutdown."

"You are wrong! It's in full operation now."

"Pardon me, sir?" The news excited Pilsung. The old man nodded several times and continued.

"Many North Korean workers still move in and out the Economic Zone. They don't work during the day, but rather do work only at night. That's why the Economic Zone looks all boarded up. That's the situation over there."

"Oh, I see," Pilsung said.

"The number of North Korean workers is growing in the Economic Zone since the shutdown of the Gaeseong Industrial Complex."

"Is that so?"

"You will be able to find her if she is working there. However..." the old man stopped talking, cleared his throat several times, and continued, "You must be very careful. You know very well who North Korean special agents are, right?"

The cellphone in his pocket vibrated quite a while but Pilsung did not feel it at all. The phone call was from Bora in Seoul. He was absorbed in conservations with them. Bora sent a text message to Pilsung, but he had not read the message. On his way back to the Tumen River Hotel, he finally read the message but he did not think it was important.

'Yeook has some information about Soon. She asks you to come back to Seoul.'

Pilsung thought he finally had a clue to find Soon. He could not trust Yeook at this point. He just passed over the message. He spoke to himself, "Maybe, Yeook made up a story for me to return to Seoul. I won't come back before I find Soon. I am sure that Soon is in the Tumen Special Economic Zone."

Pilsung recalled Soon and his last words to her on the day when the South Korean government made a decision to shut down the Gaeseong Industrial Complex. He said to her, "Escape to Yanbian."

She didn't say yes or no, but rather asked him, "Have you been in Yanbian?" Her words weighed upon his mind. He wanted to interpret them in a positive way. At least, she didn't refuse his pleas for her escape.

He replied to Bora, *'Bora, thanks so much for texting. I think I found a clue. I need to focus on what I am doing here for a while.'*

Episode 5
A Mata Hari Training

HANA enjoyed playing a double role. She took Pilsung wherever he wanted to go and reported what he had done with whom, when, and how to her boss in Seoul. He was greatly satisfied with her reports. He asked her to keep watching him. He added that she should take a chance and encourage him to return to Seoul.

Hana also had to control her customer Pilsung according to her plan. Her partner in Seoul asked her to take him to as many places as possible until she's asked to hand him over to another partner in Tumen. Her first step to control him was to get him up early in the morning. She had some problems with him to begin with. Now she works in perfect harmony with him.

Pilsung struggled to wake up early in Seoul. He actually enjoyed sleeping late. On weekends he usually stayed tucked in bed until 10 o'clock in the morning. He wanted to correct this sleeping habit. He tried many times in Seoul but always failed. Thanks to Hana's morning calls, the struggle had disappeared since coming to Tumen. He got up at six o'clock every morning. Then Hana arrived at seven o'clock at the hotel and took him to Yanji, Longjing, Baishan, and everywhere else within the Yanbian Korean Autonomous Prefecture.

Pilsung especially looked forward to visiting the Tumen Special Economic Zone. He had been looking forward to it since his visit to Jungam Village the other day. Pilsung didn't think that Hana could be the right person to help him look for Soon in the Economic Zone. She had never mentioned the place before his visit to Jungam Village. He put two and two together and decided to call the broker in Seoul. His prospect came through. With the help of the broker, he could successfully locate a Chinese officer working at the Economic Zone. The broker seemed to have great personal connections in China. Pilsung came to understand the importance of *guanxi* (關係) in China. *Guanxi* didn't only mean personalized networks, it was also closely related to money. The broker made an extra charge for the arrangement. The deal with him was simple and clear though. He called Pilsung right after he received the amount that he had asked.

"A Chinese gentleman will wait for you at four o'clock in the afternoon at Changbai Café in Tumen downtown."

"Changbai Café?"

"Yes. I will send you the address."

"You didn't say what day."

"Oh, I am sorry. He told me three days later. It will be… next Monday."

"Thanks so much. I will be there just in time."

"Make sure that no one follows you. Don't even let Hana know about your meeting with the Chinese officer. He will give you a ride to the Economic Zone."

"How long will I be able to stay there?

"I don't know exactly. Maybe a couple of hours, I guess. Is that enough for you?"

"I think so."

"You will be there as his special guest. Please don't forget that you will have to dress up."

Meanwhile, Pilsung tried to collect information on Soon from the local Koreans living there. She could have contacted at least some of them if she had been working in the Economic Zone. Hana took him wherever he wanted to visit. However, his efforts were in vain. He couldn't find anyone who could get in touch with Soon recently. She might hide herself in the Economic Zone or was not allowed to contact local Koreans in China. He didn't want to imagine, but Soon could still be somewhere in North Korea. He thought that he would take her out of the Economic Zone or North Korea by receiving help from the contact person in China. If that was the case in the Yanbian area, it was his visit to a Korean restaurant in Yanji.

After dinner, a North Korean singer sang a song's lyric, "*Love, Love, Oh My Love*". It was North Korean pop music, well-known as the theme song of *The Story of Chunhyang*. An anonymous author from around 1700s in the Chosun Dynasty wrote the tale. Famous film directors in Korea made a romance movie depicting *The Story of Chunhyang*. The North Korean singer reminded Pilsung of a heroine in the Chunhyang movies. She looked like she was in her early twenties. She had a pretty and sorrowful face.

Her singing brought out sadness in everyone in the restaurant. Pilsung immediately slipped into her song. At some point in the singing, she fixed her eyes on Pilsung and gradually moved her steps near to him. She flashed a discrete smile. She finally offered her hand to him for a dance. Pilsung stood up from his chair and held her hand. She continued her song lyric, written by a poet Cho Ryung-Chool (1913–1993).

'Love, love, oh my love,
You are like a flower.
Even more beautiful than a flower,
Oh you are my love.
On Dano day in spring, like a dream
Oh my love sent to myself.
In this air you are my love,
You are my love in that air.'

Pilsung felt her hand warm. He didn't know why but suddenly tears spilled out of his eyes. He couldn't keep time with his foot. He gave up her hand and came back to his seat. Even in a car back from Yanji to Tumen, her face lingered and her voice echoed in his mind. He couldn't forget her whispers in his ear.

"Please don't trust anybody. You could be in danger if someone knows you are looking for a North Korean girl," her voice was soft, sweet, and even attractive with her North Korean accent.

"What kind of person are you talking about?"

"They could be a North Korean secret agent or a Chinese policeman. Take care of yourself, please."

She was so kind and acting like a close friend of Soon. It was a mystery how she had known Pilsung was looking for a North Korean girl. He asked her, but she would not answer the question. Instead, she just offered a mysterious smile to him. He asked her if she knew anyone in the Tumen Special Economic Zone. She didn't answer but just stared at him with her eyes wide open. Pilsung made a mental note to visit and see her again in this Korean restaurant.

On that day, Pilsung suggested Hana take half a day off from his own time. She was reluctant to accept it but she had no choice. Pilsung had high hopes for the Tumen Special Economic Zone. He felt confident that he would be able to see Soon over there. He arrived at Changbai Café just on time. The Chinese officer showed up ten minutes later. He was a little fat around the belly and looked in his late forties. He didn't hide that he was an ethnic Korean living in China, or *Chosunjok*, who spoke Korean fluently.

"I have carefully reviewed North Korean workers' personal information a few days ago and again this morning, but I couldn't find her in our records," he observed Pilsung carefully. He had an overbearing manner about him. The news disappointed Pilsung. *However, it's too early to give up looking for Soon in the Economic Zone*, he thought.

"Thank you very much, sir. I appreciate your time and efforts. Would you please allow me to gain access to the records? I would like to double check," he tried to keep his spirits high in the face of bitter disappointment.

"No problem, at all. You may need it, because some North Korean workers use a false identity," he had the gift of gab. Pilsung found no words of reply for a little while. What if Soon uses a false identity? She will be in trouble with Chinese authorities. Pilsung won't be able to do anything at all for her.

"Oh, I see, sir. I will look up the records very carefully, and let you know if I can find any acquaintances. I heard that some Korean workers have been transferred from Gaeseong to Tumen. I would like to look around the Economic Zone, too. Please give me permission to do that."

The Chinese officer nodded his head and stood up out of his chair. They drove slowly and arrived at the Economic Zone around 5 o'clock in the afternoon. Pilsung was seated in a small office. He had a chance to look up the North Korean workers' personal information through the computer monitor. However, the personal information was not original, but a simplified one including only name, photo and address. Pilsung couldn't find Soon's record. He also had an opportunity to look around several factories in the Economic Zone. Their workplaces were very much similar to the ones in Gaeseong.

PILSUNG got ready for his morning walk. He didn't end up with nothing from his visit to the Tumen Special Economic Zone. He recognized one factory worker from his sewing factory. He didn't say anything about that to the Chinese officer though. She could be of great help to Pilsung. This morning he selected to wear navy blue shorts and white walking shoes. Blue and white are a symbol of hope and peace. He knotted a shoelace tightly. He felt light on his feet. He also had a feeling that something good would happen to him during the day. He spoke to himself as if he was hypnotizing himself.

"I will surely find Soon. She must be near me. It must be Soon that the older men mentioned when I visited Jungam Village. Come hell or high water, I won't be disappointed. I will rise again."

"Where there is a will, there is a way." He left the hotel reciting that affirmation as he walked toward Tumen downtown. Then he crossed the street where he encountered a passenger with a black plastic bag in his hand passing by. Pilsung tried to exchange nods with him but the passenger avoided eye contact. He went along the street for one more block. Some passengers came into his sight. He witnessed an interesting scene. Almost all of them had a black plastic bag in their hands.

Pilsung stood up and looked around in front of a traffic signal carefully. A big sign waited two more blocks away from his location. The sign, Tumen Wholesale Market, was written in Korean. Cars and people crowded the streets. A street market stood next to the wholesale market. He walked closer to the street market.

He heard words spoken in both Korean and Chinese. A middle-aged man with white shorts peeked around this vendor and that vendor. He tried to make eye contact with a middle-aged woman selling rice cakes behind her stall. Pilsung felt hungry and stopped walking in front of the rice cake stall.

"How much is it?" Pilsung pointed at a small rice cake box.

"Five Yuan per box."

"May I buy half a box?" A box seemed too large for him.

"Three Yuan for half a box," her answer was simple and clear.

Pilsung decided to buy a full box of rice cakes. He handed a five-Yuan bill to her. A girl next to the middle-aged woman put it in a black plastic bag and handed it to him.

"Here you are."

He took out a piece of rice cake from the box, put it in his mouth and chewed it with his mouth closed. He idly went around all the stalls on the street market.

A WOMAN ran along the street market panting and puffing. It was Hana. Without hesitation, she walked into a three-story building on the way into the street market and without a break went up to its rooftop. She found Pilsung in front of a rice cake vendor. She fixed her eyes on a girl standing behind the rice cake stall. Hana couldn't identify her easily because she lowered her head. Hana shot short videos on the scene with a high-performance camera. She hardened her face after she identified the girl through the video.

Pilsung was out of her sight in an instant, while Hana focused on the girl for a while. She quickly made a 50-meter radius circle with the rice cake vendor as its center, and looked for Pilsung. He was not in the circle. Again, she made a circle of a 100-meter radius and carefully observed individuals moving, walking, and chatting. Pilsung was there in the second circle.

A middle-aged man with white shorts was moving toward Pilsung. Hana left in a hurry as soon as she saw the man with white shorts. While Pilsung walked along the market gazing around, the man with white shorts hit Pilsung's shoulder with his. He did that on purpose.

"Oops! I am sorry, very sorry," he said in Korean and nodded his head to Pilsung.

"That's okay!" Pilsung responded to him in Korean, too.

"Oh, we both speak Korean! Are you from Korea?"

"Yes. I am from Seoul. How about you, sir?"

"I am from Suwon."

He introduced himself as a trading businessman between Korea and Yanbian. His last name was Bak. The two walked together along the street market, and stopped their walking in front of a Chinese pancake stall. Mr. Bak spoke to her in Chinese. They seemed to know each other well. She gave a piece of pancake to Pilsung and another piece to Mr. Bak. He paid cash to her with a big smile.

"What brought you here to Tumen?" asked Bak.

"Um… I am looking for work here in Tumen," he didn't tell him the truth.

"You must have fallen on hard times."

He pretended to hesitate for a moment, pulled out his business card, and handed it to Pilsung.

"Maybe I can be of help to you. Give me a call."

He tapped Pilsung's shoulder several times. Pilsung turned around and walked toward the Tumen River Hotel. Mr. Bak again headed for the rice cake vendor. Hana with a straw hat kept track of where Mr. Bak had stopped by this morning. She also bought a piece of Chinese pancake. She stopped to chat with the vendor. The vendor answered in Chinese when Hana asked questions in Korean. Hana spoke to herself. "The vendor doesn't look Chinese at all. She is Korean for sure. Then how come she pretends to be Chinese?" Hana tilted her head several times and then went in the direction Pilsung headed a few minutes ago.

RIGHT before darkness set in, Pilsung left the Tumen River Hotel and walked toward the café where Mr. Bak talked to him on the phone this afternoon. Pilsung asked him on the phone if he knew someone in Jungam Village. He knew some older men in the Village Hall very well. He also was well aware of the Sul family story. Pilsung recalled his words.

"I can be of help to you if you are looking for a girl from the Sul's family. It could be much easier to take her out of the Tumen Special Economic Zone if she has been working there. I can locate a person who can help you cross the Tumen River to North Korea. He might know where your girl lives and can help you bring her out to China again. Then you can take her to Seoul. I think I am the right person to help you."

Pilsung felt like he met a savior. For a few seconds, he also thought this man could be the third party the broker mentioned. *Was he the man? Yes, he could be.* Pilsung headed for Tumen Square first and turned right. He walked along the street until he met an intersection. Then he made a left turn at the intersection. He walked fifty steps forward. Mr. Bak was damn right. He saw the sign, Tumen River Café. A couple of women were waiting for him outside its door.

"You must be Pilsung, right? You are just on time. This way, please."

Pilsung was seated in a quiet room. Although he didn't order, a waitress delivered a beer.

"Mr. Bak called us. He will be about 30 minutes late. He asked me to deliver beers or other drinks whatever you would like. Are you okay with beers?"

Pilsung nodded. She poured the bottle into the glass and sat next to him. A sound of high heels and women chatting occasionally reached his ears. He strained to listen but couldn't catch even one word. The waitress sitting next to him talked to him whenever he tried to grasp the meaning of the chatter outside of the room. Pilsung was in a half-drunken state when Mr. Bak came into the café and sat across from him.

"Have you enjoyed your drinks? I am sure this is one of the best cafés in Tumen." He ordered more beers. Pilsung stood up and opened the door to take a restroom break. He could hear women chatting a bit more clearly. They spoke in Korean, but he couldn't understand their words. Pilsung felt as if they were speaking in code.

When Pilsung came back from the restroom, a strange girl sat next to his seat. She introduced herself to him but Pilsung couldn't remember her name. He finished a couple more bottles with her. He couldn't remember anything at all afterwards. He didn't even know when Mr. Bak left.

PILSUNG woke up lying on his back in a room in a palatial residence. The silky blanket felt so soft and smooth on his naked body. Its touch was like sweet love play. The scent of a woman was in the air. Feminine sounds reached his eardrums. The scent and the sound were somehow familiar. Pilsung sat up and looked at the girl next to him. Oh! It was Soon from his dreams.

"I have been looking for you, Soon. Where were you?"

"I miss you so much, Pilsung."

Pilsung kissed her lips. The sound of women laughing reached his ears through a crack in the door. Someone said with a soft voice, "Shh!" The laughter disappeared immediately. Instead, the voice of a beautiful, voluptuous woman flew into his room, lifted by the music of Mozart's *Clarinet Concerto*.

"The most common position leads you to the most thrilling state in lovemaking. Ancient sages gave it the highest score. Think about how a dragon flies in the sky. Its body moves up and down softly. It is a *dragon flying position* (龍翻). It is written in a classic called *Sunijin* (素女經). Now, pay attention to their movement in the room. Be silent!"

It was as if unseen forces led them to do what the woman just described. Soon was lying down on her back and Pilsung wrapped his arm under her neck. She raised her hip slightly and he pushed his back up a little. His body slid down onto hers. Their movement was soft, and so was their feeling. He felt as if he and his mate flew among the clouds. So did she.

A clarinet sound floated in the background as the concerto reached its second movement. The tone color was quiet and touchy, like their motion in their bed. They were just like a musical instrument in the concerto. When Soon moved forward with the timbre of a feeble clarinet, Pilsung responded to her with a dull horn. He seemed to unlock her secrets, and waves of pleasure engulfed her entire body. They became a pair of dragons and flew in the air. They advanced and retreated, and they flew up and down. They continued until Soon shivered with pleasure. The voice of the same voluptuous woman crept into his room again.

"The next is a *fish-scale rubbing position*. Please imagine a pair of fish in the water with one rubbing itself against its partner. You should be sitting on top of your man and keep moving your body back and forth. This is a position of giving your man a break for a while. He sure needs it after serving you diligently in the first position, doesn't he? You have to work hard for him, controlling the speed of your movement. Don't speed up too fast. Don't slow down too slow. Move your body, observing his physical and mental state. You can enjoy looking at your man full of pleasure. It depends on how technically and diligently you work on him. Go on, my girl!"

A fish scale rubbing position (魚接鱗)? She thought of it for a minute and then led him to change to the position. Now she squatted on top of him and looked down upon his face. She moved back and forth and began gradually pushing a piece of joy and pleasure deep into his body. He closed his eyes gently and felt pleasures like a torrent surging upon his whole body. "Ah," an interjection broke out from his mouth.

Pilsung raised himself into a sitting position. Soon embraced his neck with her arms. Her lips parted in a soundless scream. He licked her lips. They were soft and sweet. Both felt a thrill at the same time. They seemed to be going through mind-blowing ecstasy.

"Look at them. I didn't even ask them to change their position. They did it out of awareness, didn't they? She just followed what her body asked her to do. Their position changed from a fish scale rubbing to a *crane-neck rubbing* (鶴交傾) so naturally. She shows a natural aptitude for a celebrated *gisaeng*. Surely, she will be a second Mata Hari or a North Korean Mata Hari. What a revolution warrior she is!"

THE DARKNESS still remained in the air. It was just before sunrise. Silence sank all around. Suddenly, a dull *thud* of moving steps outside the room woke up Pilsung. Clearly Soon had been next to him last night, but had already gone now. Nobody was in the room except for Pilsung. In a hurry he picked up and put on his pants. A group of three big men, one with a mustache, one with a beard, and one with a bald head dropped in on his room without knocking. They grabbed and dragged him out, before he had even zipped up his trousers.

"Who are you?" he shouted, "What are you doing to me?"

Pilsung screamed out, but they didn't answer. None in the café came out to help him. He tried to fight back, but his efforts were in vain. They were too strong for Pilsung to do something against them.

"Help! Help me, please!" he shouted again.

Nobody came out to help him. One of them covered his mouth with a big, coarse hand. Only a shadow of a man passed by the scene soundlessly. It was Mr. Bak.

Episode 6
A Reunion

AN AIRPLANE passed through the clouds, and rolled side to side for a minute. Several passengers made a sound of fright. A stewardess in haste made an in-flight announcement to fasten seat belts. All crewmen, who were busily engaged in serving passengers, returned to their seats. After a little while, silence regained over the cabin. No sound was heard except for the engine noise of the plane.

Pilsung, keeping his eyes forward, lowered his head, held his cellphone with one hand and pressed hard on a text message with the other hand. A photo of a handwritten memo came into his sight. It was written by Soon on white paper. Tears welled in his eyes. Pilsung blinked them away. He touched it and read it again.

'...I decided to cross the river to see you ... Death would be better than life without you, Pilsung ... I love you, Pilsung. From your Soon'

"Yes, you were my Soon for sure," Pilsung muttered to himself, "You were near me in my mind day or night. You still are. You know what? At the moment when a piece of sunshine touched the back of my neck below my head covered with a black sheet, you spoke in a sweet whisper. Don't worry, Pilsung. You will be fine. Your words had indeed appeased my fear."

"Was I kidnapped?" he asked himself. "I am not sure," he answered his own question.

It was like a dream, a dramatic dream from being kidnapped by a group of North Korean agents to the flight back to Seoul. These incidents all occurred within the last 24 hours. Pilsung thought he was about to visit North Korea to see Soon. For him, it was still mystery whether or not Mr. Bak was the third person sent to him by the broker in Seoul.

Of course, Hana took Pilsung to Yanji Airport, and kept watching him pass the departure gate. Bora sent him a text message right after he got a boarding pass. The text was about Soon. He was thoroughly confused. He couldn't trust anybody. Although Hana told him about Soon, he just ignored what she said to him. He couldn't believe Bora's words, either. He called her but didn't answer the phone. Instead, a text message was delivered to him.

"Pilsung, a long story is waiting for you about Soon."

Pilsung was at a loss for words. He couldn't decode secrets behind Soon. His airplane just flew out of a cloud. Blue sky was ahead of him. Again, his last 24 hours went by in a flash.

PILSUNG was caught in the back seat of a car after being dragged by a group of strangers at dawn. They covered his face with a black sheet. His hands were tied. He recalled a scene from his memory of a man decapitated by a member of ISIS. He had watched it on TV a couple of years ago. He prayed for Soon's safety, and quietly waited for his fate.

"Tell me who you are, and why I was kidnapped," Pilsung shouted.

He turned his head from side to side and looked around, but nothing was seen, because his head was covered with a thick black sheet. No one in the car replied to his words. The man in the passenger seat turned his face to the driver.

"Drive toward Erdaobaihe!" he ordered. This man had a strong North Korean accent. He fiddled with his mustache.

"Yes, sir!"

Erdaobaihe is a small town at the foot of the Chinese side of the Baekdu Mountain, also called the Changbai Mountain by the Chinese. The town had been in boom, since lots of tourists descended on the Baekdu Mountain to take a look at a volcanic lake called *Chunji*, meaning 'lake of heaven'. Its Chinese name is *Tianci*. They were not Chinese agents, but North Korean agents. He felt relieved just a bit. Maybe he would get to visit North Korea, after all. They hadn't hurt him yet, so Pilsung was hopeful.

HANA got ready for her morning jog. She felt that time was not on Pilsung's side. She recalled a phone call with her partner in Seoul in her mind while lacing her shoes. He asked her to get ready to hand Pilsung over to his other partners in Tumen. She asked to whom and when, but he didn't give her specifics. He just said it would happen sometime within a couple of days. She became fond of him while taking him to every corner of the Yanbian Korean Autonomous Prefecture.

She finished doing warm-up exercises. Her cellphone rang right after she left her home. She stopped walking and listened to her cellphone with a serious face.

"What? He was kidnapped? Did you say the Changbai Mountain?"

She recalled the rice cake vendor in the street market. Actually, two women were selling rice cakes. One was middle aged, and the other was in her twenties. A man with white shorts was a suspicious guy too. Hana was convinced that one of them was deeply involved in the kidnapping. Hana made a call to her colleague in Baishan.

"It's early in the morning, Hana. What's up?" he asked. He seemed to be in bed. Hana explained the kidnapping specifically.

"Please stand by at a safe house of North Korean agents and wait for my next direction. We should save him before they get to Erdaobaihe. You will have to block them crossing the border between China and North Korea."

She contacted agents in Yanji and Erdaobaihe and ask them to support her to save Pilsung. She also sent three individuals' photos that she had taken on the street market in Tumen. She drove her car to the Tumen River Hotel.

THE POLICE officer received an emergency phone call around 6 o'clock in the morning. The phone call was from a secret agent in Tumen. He delivered bad news to the police officer that Pilsung had been kidnapped by a group of North Korean secret agents in Tumen. His agent found out that they did it for a ransom. According to him, they will demand a huge amount if Korean agents don't save him within 24 hours.

"Pilsung, you have made a pretty mess!"

The police officer woke up and made a phone call to a cyber-policeman who he had known for a long time. His nickname was Bundol, meaning lightning bolt. He preferred the nickname to his real name, Sooil. The police officer had done various collaborations with him. He needed Bundol's help badly at this point.

When the police officer called and let Bundol know about the kidnapping, he already knew the case. He said that he was about to call the police officer for his permission and cooperation.

"What a coincidence, Bundol! How did you know about it?"

"Please don't ask specifics. I know him personally." Bundol glanced at a dream-hacker Chulbang. Bundol was a member of Anonymous International. It is a loosely associated international network of hackers. He was asked to locate Pilsung by his members working actively across the world. A Korean Chinese hacker let him know about Pilsung's kidnapping case. He immediately invited Chulbang to his office to work together.

"We have to save him as soon as possible within 24 hours."

"Please give me the phone number of your agent in Yanji."

"You have to take an oath of secrecy in this case."

"Yes, I do, sir!"

The police officer gave him Hana's phone number instead of his secret agent's. Bundol could track Hana's movements as soon as he put Hana's number into his computer. Her cellphone was under the location tracking services. All intelligence agents were required to turn location tracking on when they were on duty.

Hana moved fast through the street market in Tumen, and returned to the Tumen River Hotel. She went up to Pilsung's room and packed up his luggage. She put his luggage in the trunk and got in the car. She then entered the expressway from Tumen through Yanji.

"She has to call Pilsung, then I can locate him more specifically. Please, please call him, Hana," Bundol said.

"Do you want me to call the police officer? I can ask him to ask her to call Pilsung," Chulbang said and turned his face to Bundol.

"She should call him because Pilsung is her customer, too," Bundol said. Bundol kept his eyes fixed on the monitor. Finally, her phone seemed to be connecting to Pilsung's. As soon as Pilsung received it, Bundol could locate him. He waited for a second.

Pilsung's phone rang in his pocket several times. The guy sitting next to Pilsung in the back seat pulled out the phone from Pilsung's pocket. He handed it to the guy with the mustache in the passenger seat. He looked at the phone number and shook his head. No one in the car answered the phone and so the phone cut off. Minutes slipped by. Pilsung's phone rang again. The guy sitting next to Pilsung again handed it to his boss in the passenger seat. He looked at the phone number and answered the phone this time.

"Thanks much, Mr. Bak."

Bundol, at last, could confirm Pilsung's exact location information on his monitor. The owner of the phone number connected to Pilsung's phone was also identified quickly. At that moment, the police officer and Yeook arrived at Sooil's office.

"He is a big-ticket item. I mean he is a sort of invaluable. Please keep him safe," Mr. Bak said.

"They will ask a huge amount of ransom," Yeook sighed deeply.

"You have done a good job. I will let you know soon," the man in the passenger seat said.

"Please let me talk to him. I have to make him calm down," Mr. Bak said.

"Answer the phone," the man in the passenger seat handed the phone to Pilsung.

"Hello?" Pilsung held the phone with tied hands.

"Pilsung, take it easy, please. You told me you have been looking for a girl whose name was…right, Soon. A group of three gentlemen in the car will help you to visit North Korea. They don't want anyone to know their route across the border between China and North Korea so you are disguised to be kidnapped. That's why your face is covered with a black sheet. They will release you as soon as you cross the border. That's what they do for their customers."

Pilsung didn't argue with him. He was just listening to what Mr. Bak said to him. He didn't say even a word.

"Are you following me?"

"Please, continue."

"You can call me whenever you want. They will let you talk to me on the phone. I hope you can see your girl in North Korea." Mr. Bak hung up the phone. Momentarily, Pilsung thought Mr. Bak could be the third party that the broker mentioned in Korea. Pilsung was about to ask who sent him, but Mr. Bak didn't give him a chance to ask.

"Pilsung met his match today."

"What does that mean?"

"Did you hear how good he was at speaking? The guy who called Mr. Bak is a repatriation broker to North Korea. I mean Pilsung can visit North Korea, but his safety can't be ensured," Bundol said.

The police officer handed a memo with several phone numbers to Bundol. He seized their movements on his monitor as soon as he put in the phone number. The police officer and Bundol ordered all drivers to corner the car where Pilsung was en route, and to encircle it just before the car entered Erdaobaihe. The police officer gave his last words to them.

"No gun fighting allowed. We need to write this up as a car accident."

North Korean agents had driven the car for a couple of hours. They took local roads rather than the expressway from

Tumen to Yanji. Pilsung didn't know how long he had been in the car. He could feel strong sunshine on his neck. The car reduced its speed. Suddenly, it crashed with another car. Pilsung felt like he was in a car accident. In the instant the driver got out of the car on Pilsung's side, a bunch of individuals dropped in and controlled them in a second. He heard a familiar sound.

"Pilsung, are you okay?"

Pilsung didn't say anything at all. He was so confused. He actually didn't know what was going on around him. In addition, he couldn't trust her when Hana told him everything on the way from the scene to the safe house.

"You have to get ready for the trip back to Seoul. I had a phone call from a police officer and Yeook. They told me that a girl is waiting for you in Seoul. I am sure that she is the person you have been looking for."

He thought their talks were fish baits to bring him back to Seoul. He thought he was about to visit North Korea. Pilsung didn't ask Hana any questions about Soon.

BORA looked up the arrival information board. She read the sign that the airplane from Yanji had just arrived. Bora turned her face to Soon. She kept wiping up tears from her eyes.

"Thank you. Thank you so much, Bora."

"It was a misunderstanding. Pilsung is just a friend to me. He is not my boyfriend, but a *namsachin*."

"What is *namsachin*?"

Bora explained its meaning. The word is an abbreviation of three words, *namja* meaning a male, *saram* indicating a person, and *chingu* referring to a friend. Soon laughed loudly and nodded her head.

On that day, when Soon saw Pilsung walking with Bora on the backstreets, she decided to leave Seoul. She felt that she had to. She thought Bora was his new girlfriend. She felt betrayed by his defection. Indeed, it was heartbreaking. She didn't say anything about it to the police officer. She hid herself in a small room and lived on air for a couple of days.

Then she just called him and told him that she wanted to leave Seoul.

The police officer told her not to leave for Jeju Island, but he couldn't change her mind. He said that her ID laundering was almost complete so it would be better for her to stay in Seoul. She wouldn't listen to the police officer at all. He suggested to meet with Yeook before she left for Jeju Island. She refused it. Her words were absolute.

"I will stay at Jeju Island where none will recognize me. Please help me stay there."

Soon flew to Jeju and found a job in a lamb skewers restaurant on Baojien Street, also known as Jeju China Town. She could speak Chinese fluently and was welcomed in several restaurants.

Bora visited Soon's restaurant early this morning. Soon recognized Bora right away when she came in the restaurant. *Why did she come here?* Soon recalled her with Pilsung. *To get me here in Jeju?* Soon was so afraid of having a big quarrel with Bora over Pilsung. She was not ready at all. "Who told her I am here?" She just wanted to escape from the scene.

However, Soon had no choice but to face her. She had to, otherwise what else could she do? She calmly stepped toward Bora's table and tried to take her order. "Are you ready…" Soon couldn't keep taking orders from Bora because Bora suddenly stood up and held Soon's hands with hers. Bora said to Soon, "I came here to meet you for Pilsung."

"For Pilsung? What about him?" she responded with hostility, readying herself for a quarrel with Bora.

"Everything has been settled for you and Pilsung."

Soon was so confused momentarily, and replied, "What? Say that again?"

Bora kept her cool, "I am here to take you to Seoul."

"I was so frightened as soon as I saw you at the restaurant," Soon said.

"I was scared that you might run away from me," Bora responded.

"I think Pilsung is coming out."

Pilsung came into Soon's sight first. Then Bora recognized him passing by the gate. Soon couldn't move and just fixed her eyes on Pilsung. Pilsung stopped walking and looked at Soon for a moment. Soon didn't even blink. She was afraid of missing him again. Bora raised her hand to him welcoming him back. Pilsung ran into Soon's arms.